The Duke of Entenhausen

Simon Alce

The Duke of Entenhausen

& 11 more short stories about
economists, lovers and
even normal people

Simon Alce is a German literary figure. His imagination of what might possibly happen behind closed doors has helped shape a wonderful first collection of 12 charming short stories about economists, bureaucrats, lovers and even normal people.

Disclaimer:
All characters, events, places and institutions in these stories are 100% fictional. Any resemblance to actual people, past events or real institutions is completely coincidental. Especially, the "big international organization" does not exist.

Bibliographical Information of the Deutsche Nationalbibliothek
This publication is listed in the Deutsche Nationalbibliographie of the Deutsche Nationalbibliothek; detailed bibliographical information can be accessed under http: //dnb.d-nb.de

© 2013 Simon Alce
Illustrations by JOCI
Layout, printing and publication:
BoD – Books on Demand

ISBN: 978-3-7322-6371-4

Index

Pull and Post

Behaviour and actions do not happen without motivation. Scientists commonly agree that the sources of motivation fall more specifically into the category of a push motivation (an internal disposition) or a pull motivation (an external incentive). "Emergence" is the perspective that the brain's neuronal processes generate psychological feelings. These feelings can motivate individuals into action.

It happened at the time when the post offices were still state-owned and the delivery of letters was under law a protected monopoly. I entered the post office of the 9th district of Vienna. It did not come as a surprise that I would have to wait for a while – there were at least twenty people queuing up. I wondered why only one counter was open, given the number of clients and that two clerks were sitting behind signboards with the word "closed" on it. The next fifteen minutes I spent drowsing in the slowly moving waiting line but suddenly I was rudely awakened from my daydream. The two other clerks had finished their break and the zealous crowd rushed to the opened counters. I realized that I moved up to number three in my line. From where I was standing I could follow what was happening at the desk. A pretty blonde lady held a bunch of letters in her hands.

Pretty Lady (with a warm charming voice): *"I have some letters to mail. May I hand them over to you?"*

Clerk (unfriendly): *"Do you have any stamps?"*

Pretty Lady: *"No, I haven't. I wanted to ask you whether you could take my letters as they are and use your stamping machine."*

Clerk: *"How many?"*

Pretty Lady: *"I think there are 96."*

Clerk: *"Not possible. You have to buy the stamps."*

Pretty Lady (a bit less charming): *"May I ask you why? To glue 96 stamps on 96 letters is not so much of a fun."*

Clerk (very unfriendly now): *"It needs a minimum of 100 for the stamping machine."*

Pretty Lady (disappointed): *"Okay, 96 stamps then."*

Clerk (using the calculator): *"7 each, equals 672 Schilling."*

In this very moment I had to take a decision. Of course, I scented the pleasure to help Pretty Lady to stick all these stamps on the letters. But sometimes it is also a pleasure to show that you are smart. For what other reason would I have studied economics? I spotted the classical case for a factor substitution (labor against capital). So I instinctively intervened from behind.

Me: *"May I make a suggestion?"*

Clerk (surprised): *"What is it?"*

Me: *"I am happy to pay for the four additional pieces. We arrive at the magic number of 100 and you can use the stamping machine."*

Clerk: *"That does not work."*

Me: *"May I ask why?"*

Clerk: *"I need 100 physical letters for the stamping machine, not only a payment."*

Me: *"You could perhaps just use some old used envelopes?"*

Clerk: *"That does not work. This would be against our rules."*

9

I had obviously reached a point of no return. Driven by "emergence" I just had to get the letters of Pretty Lady into the machine, even if the benefits of factor substitution would sharply deteriorate.

Me: *"But I am sure that it is not against the rules that I buy four new envelopes and you add them to the 96?"*

Clerk: *"If you bring me 100 letters I can make use of the stamping machine."*

Me: *"I thought I may buy them from you. This is a post office, isn't it?"*

Clerk: *"The counter to buy envelopes is on the other side."*

Pretty Lady and I hastily turned around. There were at least 15 people waiting. We fell into loud laughter.
Pretty Lady (turning to me): *"This looks very much like 96 licks."*

Me: *"48 each if you like. But preferably in the coffee shop next door."*

Perhaps I should have been more thankful to the Vienna post office. But it came very strongly into my mind that – apart from the unique offer to use the waiting lines as an efficient platform for conversation – some things could improve (e.g. the service). On the next occasion I spoke to the minister, who in the meantime had become a big boss within a big international organization.

Big Boss: *"Did I get you right?"*

Me: *"You did. I asked you for the responsibility for the liberalization of postal services."*

Big Boss: *"You are the first cabinet member who volunteered for that job."*

Me: *"Miller just performed an exciting jig when I told him that I would be happy to take over from him."*

Big Boss: *"But why do you want to do that? Do you have a fever?"*

Me: *"Not at all. I am only convinced that the sector needs some competition."*

Big Boss: *"This dossier brings nothing but trouble. For every little step away from the monopoly we turn hundreds of thousands of postmen into enemies. I still fail to understand why you consider this appealing."*

I reported my adventure in the postal office in Vienna.

Me: *"I have a very strong pull motivation."*

Big Boss: *"A what….? What happened with the Lady?"*

Me: *"We are still in touch, mostly by writing letters."*

Big Boss: *"I understand. A double pull motivation so to speak."*

The Big Boss smiled and indeed asked me to develop a draft proposal for the liberalization of postal services. After a painful period of adjustment inside the big international organization, the Big Boss decided to put the proposal on the agenda of the decision making body of the big international organization. It suggested a phasing out of any monopoly for postal services. The proposal was however never adopted. In the same week, the big international organization for which we worked had to step down. A member of the board had a problem with an overpaid agent, and the problem created a strong pull motivation for the Parliament to push the colleague out of the job.

I cheered myself up and married Pretty Lady. She left Austria and moved in with me. At the same time my interest in the quality of postal services has considerably declined.

The Lady Bird Tie

Status symbols are perceived, visible signs of one's social position and indicators of economic or social status. Products that can be bought by wealth, such as cars, houses, or fine clothing are considered status symbols in a commercial society. In academic circles, a list of publications in recognized journals and a securely tenured position at a prestigious university are a mark of high status. In the big international organization it is all about windows and parking spaces.

The parking issue is quite straightforward. The only question is whether an official has the privilege of a reserved space. It allows one to sleep longer in the mornings while all the others have to come ahead of others to grab one of the few non-reserved spaces left in the garage or, alternatively, manage the hostesses from the Commune waiting outside to fine those who missed paying for the public parking. People at the very top level of the big international organization can also reserve a parking space for their secretary or, if they have two, for both of them. This is the ultimate symbol of importance and status but below that level there are only two classes: officials who have a good night's rest and those who have to run to the parking meter.

Windows and office spaces offer many more possibilities to differentiate among officials. Obviously, a symbol only works if it is widely recognized and in some cases the people concerned probably overestimate their importance. However, the number of windows is the indisputable status symbol for an official working with the big international organization. The administration holds a detailed list of who has the right to how many windows and watches it like holy cows. Promotions and reorganizations are usually followed by significant conversions of the offices and quite frequently, staff have to share one office in order to create new possibilities to add windows for somebody who has been freshly promoted.

Thomas Ergenzinger was born into an Eldorado of status symbols. He came from Austria where all sorts of titles indicate the status of a person. Until the year 1919, civil servants were quite frequently awarded with the nobility title "Edler", ranking just beneath a "Ritter" (Knight). After the nobility titles were abolished in that year, other titles like academic degrees (Magister, Doctor) or job titles (like "Hofrat" or "Parlamentsrat") took their place. The Austrians liked these titles so much that the population extended their use to family members. When Thomas spent some days in a hotel in Tyrol his French wife was addressed with "Doctor Ergenzinger" and any attempt from her side to stop this nonsense was constantly ignored. Ergenzinger was shocked when he started working with the big international organization. Titles did not matter at all, everything was about the windows. Furthermore, following a mysterious and inconsistent rule, the powerful cabinet members had very tiny offices with only two small windows. Thomas started to realize that the big international organization was quite special, at least from an Austrian point of view.

But some time later, something happened that changed his mind.

Thomas was not without a sense of humor. Occasionally, he enriched his interventions at meetings with funny comments. This time a new young colleague had joined the meeting between the cabinets. The new guy had not yet said anything, but Thomas noticed that he wore a conspicuous yellow tie with some red ladybird beetles on it. Some minutes later his boss entered with almost the same tie, just the markings of the ladybird beetles were a bit different.

Thomas had the floor and was speaking about some issues on the agenda, but when he saw the two colleagues talking to each other he couldn't hold back. He continued to speak in the same voice without any break and said: *"….by the way, I admire our Dutch colleagues for their wonderful yellow ladybird ties. It looks like such a chic team outfit that I'm considering to change the cabinet."*

People around the table were laughing loudly, including the interpreters who had translated everything. As the two concerned were immersed in their conversation and Thomas seamlessly continued with his technical intervention they did not notice why everybody was laughing. The meeting ended a few minutes later with nothing special happening. But when Thomas entered his office the very next morning, he found a yellow tie with red ladybird beetles on the back of his chair. There was also a little sheet of paper with a handwritten message. Thomas read:

"Dear colleague! Unfortunately, I missed some parts of your intervention yesterday. I was only told by someone about what you said later. Actually, I think you are very well where you are but since you like the ladybird tie that much, I have allowed myself the honor to make this little gift. Constantijn."

Thomas read it twice and could still not believe it. But he was even more amazed when he learnt from the official meeting report that the new fellow was nobody else than Constantijn van Oranje-Nassau, a son of the Queen of the Netherlands.

Thomas wondered whether he would have had this wonderful adventure had he known with anticipation whom he was joking with. If he was honest, Thomas doubted that he would have commented on the tie of a real prince. His conclusion was that not every status symbol was necessarily as helpful as a reserved parking space. If other people are awed by a title of noblesse or a huge ten windows office they might not dare to show their human side.

If you happen to visit the big international organization and you see a guy wearing a yellow tie with red ladybird beetles on it, this may be Hofrat Doctor Thomas Ergenzinger. None of his titles figure on his business card, not even in the German version. Instead, he wears the royal tie quite frequently, which reminds him of what really matters.

The Bad Economist

As much as he tried, Rudolfo simply could not agree with Vanessa. It had been just against everything he believed. According to Rudolfo, good economists had to be paranoid.

In the old days, economics were part of more general philosophical questions. Scientists like Bernard Mandeville, John Stuart Mill or Adam Smith looked at the interaction of private and public benefit and there was a lot of debate about the (philosophical) question: to what extent people should be allowed to follow their own objectives (e.g. whether they should not do so if the utility of their actions were negative for the community). Modern economics has however given up on the idea that economics should be a "moral science". Today's economists were collectively hiding behind Adam Smith's term of the "invisible hand of the market" and thought that the relevance of ethics could be denied. Rudolfo Colomer was a post-modern Chicago school economist. In this tradition, he was taught to understand and develop econometric models that were based on individual utility-maximization. His professional views found their way into his private thinking. The case of Fatima was a classic. In fact, he could not disagree more with Vanessa.

Fatima came to their house every Tuesday to iron the laundry. She had excused herself for the next six weeks due to other obligations (the museum she worked with hosted a special exhibition which required her presence). Therefore she would not be able to do the ironing at their house. But

Fatima offered to pick up the laundry, do the work at her own place and bring it back.

Vanessa: *"She isn't letting us down. Isn't that lovely?"*

Rudolfo: *"Wait a minute. The story could be invented. Maybe we're just paying too much and she has decided to engage a subcontractor."*

Vanessa: *"What?"*

Rudolfo: *"She picks up the laundry, gives it to someone else and pays that person let's say 20 Euros. But as she charges us 40, she's left with a profit of 20 Euros."*

Vanessa: *"I can't imagine that she would do something like that and she would have to come here twice to pick up and deliver."*

Rudolfo: *"Didn't you tell me that her daughter works with the police and is on patrol with the police car?"*

Vanessa: *"So what? Why is it relevant?"*

Rudolfo: *"If the daughter agrees with the colleague in the car that the police patrol also has to cover our street, Fatima may pass on the transportation cost to the taxpayer. Ideally the daughter delivers the laundry directly to the subcontractor and picks it up again once it is ready. There are no opportunity costs of time. All in all she makes a profit of 100%."*

Vanessa: *"You are unbelievable. I refuse to believe that."*

Rudolfo Colomer looked warmly at his wife. He loved Vanessa for her loyalty to Fatima and deep inside he was hoping that he was wrong. On the other hand, that very day he had just experienced another case where economic theory was right. Rudolfo worked with a big international organization and had tried to change a flight for a business trip.

In economics, the "principal–agent problem" (or "agency dilemma") concerns the difficulties in motivating one party (the agent), to act in the best interests of another (the principal) rather than in his or her own interests. In fact, the problem potentially arises in almost any context where one party is being paid by another to do something, whether in formal employment or a negotiated deal such as paying for dentists or car repairs. The two parties have different interests and asymmetric information (the agent having more information), such that the principal cannot directly ensure that the agent is always acting in his or her (the principal's) best interests, particularly when activities that are useful to the principal are costly to the agent, and where elements of what the agent does are costly for the principal to observe.

When his secretary told him the price for his business trip to Riga, Rudolfo Colomer checked alternatives and found one that was 400 Euros cheaper than the offer from the travel agency. It was not a direct flight, so Rudolfo would need to stop over in Frankfurt and would arrive three hours later. The secretary asked him to discuss the matter directly with the administration.

Rudolfo: *"How is the agency calculating its fee? Is it calculated as a percentage of the fare the airline is charging for the journey?"*

Administrator: *"That is the common practice."*

Rudolfo: *"And most probably the agency receives a discount from one or two air carriers also as a percentage, but progressively in relation of its yearly turnover."*

Administrator: *"That I do not know. What do you need Mr. Colomer?"*

Rudolfo: *"The agency has a double self-interest to sell the ticket it just issued. First of all, it makes more money because it sells the more expensive ticket and by the end of the year it receives a discount in per cent from the air carrier. Only a radical accumulation of tickets from the same airline creates the sufficient level of turnover to be eligible for the program."*

Administrator: *"Why are you so concerned about this?"*

Rudolfo: *"I want to save taxpayers money. Please exchange the ticket. Return flight via Frankfurt, 400 Euro less."*

Administrator (disbelieving): *"You want to save taxpayers' money?"*

Rudolfo listened into the silence. He knew that there was still something to come. As the big international organization was a very modern, reformed organization, the administration was well prepared to handle the agency dilemma of its officials.

Administrator: *"The return flight via Frankfurt departs two hours later than the direct flight. So you are longer at the mission's location than necessary."*

Rudolfo: *"This is without consequence for the big international organization. The arrival time for both flights is after 6:00 p.m. So I am not supposed to go to the office and work after the arrival of the direct flight."*

Administrator: *"But your flight via Frankfurt arrives after 10:00 p.m. which would give you the right to take a taxi from the airport. And your mission would be longer compared to the situation using the direct flight. This would result in a higher daily allowance."*

Rudolfo: *"I suppose the 30 Euros for a taxi leaves us still with a benefit of 370 Euros for the budget. And if the daily allowance for a mission would be indeed 120 Euros per hour, the Director General would not have searched two weeks to find a volunteer for that mission."*

Administrator: *"You have to fill in the forms RT 443a and RT 443b. We will then assess the case."*

Rudolfo: *"But by then the cheaper flight might no longer be available."*

Administrator: *"Those are the rules."*

Rudolfo wondered whether economic research had already spotted that there might be cases of double principal agent problems such as the agent not only being the agent but also the principle. However, it was clear that somebody who wanted to act outside the normal routine was not welcome and likely to be treated as a criminal suspect. Rudolfo reflected a few moments. He imagined all the red tape the administrator would produce to disclose a hidden agenda and prevent him to use an official mission to achieve a private benefit.

Rudolfo: *"Okay, okay. I give up. Just leave everything as it is."*

Administrator: *"Very wise, Mr. Colomer. Thank you."*

Some time ago, a close friend of Rudolfo had introduced him to an American. The friend just mentioned that Jack was in the investment business and might be interested in hiring a good economist. Between the main course and dessert, Jack spoke about his life. As usual, Jack did not say very much. But it became clear that the profession of an investor was much easier than the work in a big international organization. Jack sipped his wine and said:

"There are so many chances out there, you know. You just have to grab them."

In that moment Rudolfo renamed Jack as "Grab'em". Beyond that, Rudolfo had not taken the matter very seriously. Grab'em was not really impressive and the salaries the big international organization paid to its officials were not bad. Thus, nothing had really happened after this first conversation. But some days before Rudolfo's friend had called and said that Jack was back in town. He would be happy to invite them to the famous "I due Signori".

The restaurant was known as one of the most exclusive Italian restaurants in Europe. Ladies got a menu without prices and the bills bore – not without any sense of humor - the meaningful inscription "take it easy". Grab'em was the last guest to arrive. Rudolfo was struck by how quickly the owner rushed from the hindmost corner of the restaurant to the front to warmly hug the arriving guest. During the main course Grab'em told him that he had an office in Manhattan but that he lived in Connecticut. Because there was nothing else to talk about at that moment, Rudolfo asked him whether he had already met Ivan Lendl there. At the time all tennis experts knew about Ivan's stately home in Connecticut. The papers reported constantly that the champion has given instructions to build a number of tennis courts in the garden, one of them with the original lawn of Wimbledon – the only grand slam tournament Ivan had not yet won (and he never did despite the fact that he had practiced in front of his door).

Grab'em was not at all surprised: *"Actually, I have visited his house in Connecticut. I like all the tennis courts and the fitness machines he had. But finally, my wife thought that it would not suit us."*

Instantly, Rudolfo got a bit more curious about Jack. When

he got home he rushed to the PC and consulted the internet. Grab'em was one of the four owners of one of the top hedge funds in the whole world. Only in the past year he personally earned 300 million dollars; his assets were estimated to be above 2 billion.

It was late but he found Vanessa still awake reading in bed.

Rudolfo: *"I have to admit that I am a bad economist. For hours and hours I am sitting next to a billionaire – and I do not realize it."*

Vanessa: *"You mean Grab'em is not just talking – he really grabs?"*

Rudolfo: *"Indeed. So far, he grabbed 2 billion. It seems that there are quite a number of chances out there."*

Vanessa: *"Does he want to hire you?"*

Rudolfo: *"He had indeed thrown out some hints before we got to the Lendl story. But I completely misjudged him. I was far from showing any interest."*

Vanessa could not avoid a laughing attack. It took some time until she pulled herself together.

Vanessa: *"It is not at all true that you are a bad economist, Rudolfo."*

Rudolfo was unable to establish a link between the laughing

fit and this statement, which to him sounded like mere irony.

Vanessa: *"You were perfectly right about Fatima. I asked the retired neighbour to watch out for a police car picking up our laundry. Bingo. And the ironing is not of the same quality. Double bingo."*

Rudolfo: *"But why are you laughing?"*

Vanessa: *"You are just a little step away from achieving the target of any good economist – which is to become enormously rich. You only need to transfer your proven analytical skills in reference to the business plans of travel agents and cleaning ladies over to people where it really matters."*

Economics by the Sunglasses

At the time when I started to study economics, students were taught that economic actors are very rational people. Most models were based on the artificial character of "homo economicus". I'll spare the details here but I am quite sure that homo economicus was not the sort of person a woman would like to go out with. Or would anybody fall for a guy who pretends to know everything and only takes (without exception) rational decisions? Sometime later economists must have had mercy with the boring homo economicus and taught him to play. He found himself in prisoners' dilemmas, chicken games or other situations where he knew much less than before. Without a doubt, he suddenly looked a little bit less arrogant but it is also fair to say that his new gambling skills were not enough to make him something like a Latin lover. Still he remained absolutely rational and was even prepared to sell his own grandmother if only the price was right.

In the wake of the past financial crisis, things changed rather dramatically. Market actors proved themselves to be much less rational than expected. There was strong evidence that investors just liked to buy what others bought, they liked to sell what others sold and they liked to own what others owned. "Herding" became something like a number one hit in economic theory. It was no surprise that, also, politicians and regulators became very keen to develop new ideas on how one could stop market participants herding collectively over the cliff, especially when these investors were bankers, using savers' deposits to invest in assets which are worth a million one day and nothing the next. It was the time when the old fashioned fellows who grew up with the "homo economicus" had to forget what they had learnt.

The first meeting of the new working group took place in New York. It had cleared up after a period of grey weather and rain. My return flight was scheduled for the evening, so I found some time for a nice walk in the city. When I got out of the subway I could not believe my eyes. Thousands of beautiful girls were out there in Manhattan and without any doubt most of them seemed to have waited impatiently for this first day of summer sun to wear the sexiest outfit they could probably find.

Different from the homo economicus, an economist may be a real man. Inspired by the promising perspectives I decided to buy a pair of sunglasses. Clearly, it was far from rational to visit any shop near to Manhattan's 5th Avenue. The shop owners knew exactly where their business was located and they did not hesitate to charge prices comparable to the size of the skyscrapers around. In my defense I may only bring forward that I tried to limit the financial damage by asking the shop assistant for the cheapest model, but still the glasses were 340 dollars. I had never been known as the type who buys over-priced exclusive brands but at the very moment of my purchase I was quite happy with myself. I had followed my instinct and my instinct had told me that I wanted to watch all these gorgeous girls just waiting outside.

It was not part of my intention but during the following ten minutes I had probably learnt more about „herding" than during the whole meeting I attended the day before. As for me, nothing compares to introspection. When I stepped outside the shop I immediately understood the principle of herding, which is known as the most spectacular schooler voyaging ocean-wide in groups of thousands to hundreds of thousands. The phenomenon of schooling is not yet fully understood, but instinctively I felt that it must have something to do with predator confusion. Instead of enjoying myself I felt terribly distracted. Have you ever seen herrings traveling the ocean in groups of thousands and hundreds of thousands? Held together by invisible bonds and following invisible streams? They always appear like a huge, elegant, glittering body that glides through the sea. Like there are probably too many targets for a shark to make an optimal catch of herring, there were just too many beautiful girls in Manhattan to make a good decision on which one to gaze at. I gave up rather quickly and enjoyed a good steak in a restaurant without any windows to the street.

While I was embarking the aircraft I bumped into a member of the working group. He was known as one of the big thinkers of economic modeling and many colleagues admired him for his mathematical skills.

Big Thinker: *"I had a discussion with Turner from the U.S. this afternoon"* (Turner is another big thinker even in the eyes of the Big Thinker).

Me: *"And what did Turner say?"*

Big Thinker: *"We agreed that we will model herding."*

Me: *"You … (surprised) want to model herding?"*

Big Thinker: *"There is nothing Turner can't model"* (actually he meant there is nothing that he can't model, but he did not say).

Me (a bit hesitant to ask): *"And do you already have some ideas on how to do it?"*

Big Thinker: *"Of course. The model will be based on non-local interactions. It will consist of a long range attraction and repulsion. If the density dependence in the repulsion term will be of a higher order than in the attraction term the herd has a constant interior density with sharp edges. We will carry out linear stability analysis for the edges of the herd."*

Me: *"Very impressive."*

Big Thinker (compassionate): *"And where have you been this afternoon?"*

Me: *"I have bought a pair of sunglasses and conducted a field study."*

Big Thinker: *"A field study?"*

Me: *"Indeed. And I can already tell you without any mathematical support: Herding is expensive."*

The Duke of Entenhausen

Barney Cutter worked in the private office of the President of a big international organization. He chaired a number of important meetings and on these occasions we would meet. Without doubt, he was a very good looking fellow and on top of that he managed his meetings with eloquence and charm. I looked up to him as other people look up to pop stars and I barely dared to say more than a flowery phrase when we met in the elevator or near the coffee shop.

One day Barney appeared at the tennis club. His partner had not turned up and I was just around. So he asked me whether I would want to be the substitute. Barney did not have a lot of time to think about it, but somehow he must have had different expectations of the outcome of our tennis. During the match he complained loudly about his performance and it is no understatement when I say that he was swearing like a trooper. After a while I started to wonder about his game plan – comparable with the well-known Swedish champion Stefan Edberg, he barely played anything else than serve and volley. Different from Edberg, Barney's serve seemed however not to work that well. Instead of considering the fact that he did not win a lot of points he repeatedly yelled *"Barney, move your butt!"* and kept on running forward to be passed by the next shot. I concluded that Barney must be a man of principle – a very rare species at the top level of the big international organization. We decided to become friends. It was Barney's first step on the way to becoming the Duke of Entenhausen.

Years passed and Barney had left the big international organization to start a career in the private sector. Of course he was hired by a big international enterprise and of course he only worked in the best places. It did not come as a big surprise to me that he finally reached the position of the Chief Executive Officer of one of the subsidiaries of the big international enterprise. His private life seemed however to be less blooming – Barney admitted that he felt a bit lonely between all his employees, board meetings and business deals. I suggested introducing him to a friend of mine who was single at the time.

She lived in my home town somewhere in the Black Forest. It is really a small town. I thought that for an Englishman like Barney who had lived in London, Paris and Rome it must somehow feel like being in Entenhausen (which is the German name for "Ducksburg", the home of Donald Duck) and wisely arranged the "rendezvous" in a bigger town on the other side of the Black Forest. The plan worked. When I saw them the next morning at breakfast, Brigit Buck and Barney Cutter were already holding hands. From now on I was not needed anymore – I only got a number of postcards from Rome, Paris or London, telling me that things had turned out to be serious.

In a very short time life had changed for Barney rather dramatically. Brigit Buck was running a family owned company and obviously didn't want to give up her job and independence. Instead of preparing his meetings, Barney tortured himself by inventing hundreds of plans on how to meet his new love as often as he could. The best thing which came to his mind was to quit the job in Italy, to marry Brigit Buck and move to Entenhausen.

To be a "matchmaker" is nice but it also comes along with a feeling of responsibility. According to some, an Englishman in New York is already an alien. So what about an Englishman in Entenhausen? When Barney called me to tell me the news I felt that some key elements of his plan deserved a discussion.

Me: *"Are you sure you want to move to Entenhausen?"*

Barney: *"Absolutely sure."*

Me: *"There are basically three issues you should know about."*

Barney: *"I am listening."*

Me: *"First, Brigit Buck does not cook and you are English. There must be something with your genes. So she doesn't cook and you can't. You got me?"*

Barney: *"Oh my god! And the second issue?"*

Me: *"The car. What really matters in Entenhausen is your car."*

Barney: *"Why is that an issue?"*

Me: *"Come on Barney! You have the wrong brand. And the old fellow must be more than 20 years old now. If you slam the door the whole car will fall into pieces. I would urgently consider buying a new one before you cross the German border."*

As already demonstrated in tennis, Barney was a man of principle. Furthermore, the roots of his family were somewhere in Scotland. Barney had not even given up using his old jalopy when he became a Big Boss.

Barney (groaning): *"And the last issue?"*

Me: *"After cars, real estate ranks number two in Entenhausen. It is almost equally important."*

Barney (eased): *"Nothing wrong with that."*

Me: *"Wait a minute. Don't dream of getting away with an apartment in Entenhausen like you did in Paris. You need to buy a big house with a huge garden."*

Barney: *"Still nothing wrong with that. Sounds like a good investment."*

Me: *"The bad news is that you will be in charge of the lawn. In Entenhausen this is definitely a man's job. And there are no exceptions."*

There was silence at the other end – I started to imagine how hard Barney must have been breathing.

Barney (gasping): *"Are you sure?"*

Me: *"Absolutely."*

A few months later I received the invitation to the wedding. It took place on neutral territory, half way between England and Entenhausen in the South of France. Barney had asked me to be his best man and I took the pleasure to address the wedding party. I detailed on our earlier conversation and my three issues of concern. But I did not fail to tell the audience that I had personally visited Entenhausen and convinced myself that everything was fine. The only moment of second thoughts invaded me on highway 81 after Barney had picked me up from the airport. Obviously he had already inhaled enough air in Entenhausen and felt a strong desire to demonstrate that the dashed stripes in the middle of the highway can turn into one continuous line if he drove his new car at its maximum speed (I panicked a bit given the fact that these English guys are told by their government not to drive faster than only 112 km/hour and always on the wrong side). In these most fearful moments I hallucinated that I might have overdone it with my story of the Entenhausen car maniacs and that the moment when the Lord would settle accounts with me had anxiously arrived.

But that was definitely the only moment of doubt. All the other things were just perfect and I developed the theory that I should rather open an office for international marriage-broking to foster European integration than trying to do so with such ugly things as directives or regulations. The best examples were the dinners at their new house. In the beginning I was a bit skeptical. But Barney is a brilliant economist and had reanimated the idea of his famous compatriot Adam Smith who once analyzed the "division of labor". Barney's part was a huge investment in the most modern and probably most beautiful kitchen in town and – a little bit similar to the friends of Tom Sawyer who once lined up to paint Aunt Polly's garden fence – the experts among Brigit's friends volunteered to cook their favorite and most delicious meals. I think Adam Smith would have been proud of Barney and so was I. Never before had I known more people in Entenhausen (Adam Smith aimed at analyzing growth) and some of them even became close friends.

There was only one small detail where Barney left some scope for improvement. First of all I have to say that Barney had really tried very hard to revolutionize Entenhausen's philosophy on who had to mow the lawn on Saturday mornings. Instead of bothering himself with an electric lawn mower he recalled that England was at the origin of industrialization and ordered a robot from the internet. His hope was that the robot would do the job all alone by itself while Barney was reading the newspapers. Unfortunately, his robot was not "Made in Germany" and performed badly by constantly cutting its own wire. And so instead of reading the Saturday papers Barney spent a lot of time negotiating with the distributor.

I ended my wedding speech by saying that we obviously have to combine our strengths in Europe. This was something my President and other big shots from the very big international organization constantly repeated. I am not sure whether many people are really listening these days. But maybe they would if they only knew the lovely story of the Duke of Entenhausen.

Party at the Slaves Table

Italians are good hosts, this is almost a legend. They drove us from Rome to Spoleto in a fleet of black limousines, escorted by the police with a number of over-sized motor bikes chasing away everybody who could have slowed down our journey. It was July and baking hot. We started with lunch at 1:00 p.m. and ended probably more than five hours later. Of course there was a prime table with all the ministers and other VIPs and a separate table for the hard working slaves that had to prepare the conclusions. I was seated next to the restaurant owner's daughter Valeria – she was almost as tall as me (I am very tall) and spoke not one single word of anything else but Italian.

I was quite young at the time but had already experienced that my language skills would develop dramatically under favorable conditions. So I decided to share some sparkling wine with her. As a somewhat natural side effect I slipped into a light-headed mood. The day was just perfect. Valeria was funny and I probably was too, thanks to all my freshly learnt Italian. During the course of the hours it came pretty close to her jumping on my lap. In the weakest moment I accepted Valeria's invitation to play on the piano which was standing just behind us in the adjoining room. I am the boogie man.

When I returned to the slaves' table I was welcomed with enthusiastic applause (the others, notwithstanding that they were able to communicate in English, obviously had some share of sparkling drinks too). Of course I was flattered but right after this very short moment of joy I felt a cold hand on my shoulder. I turned around - it was my minister. Ministers normally prefer to talk to other ministers and indeed I had barely ever spoken a word to him before. I immediately started to develop a theory that I had probably overdone it with the entertainment offered to the audience and expected to be ordered to discipline (or even to forget my career in the public service: the minister was a German!). But then we had the following conversation:

Minister: *"I see you are amusing yourself."*

Slave/Me: *"Yes, Minister. Valeria invited me to play and she is the daughter of the host. So I could not refuse."*

Minister (looking at some empty bottles on the Slaves' table): *"Apart from your musical contribution there is obviously some other amusement too."*

Slave: *"We are in Italy, Minister."*

Minister (changing his physiognomy from very serious German into (let's say half) Italian: *"Could you do me a favor?"*

Slave: *"That is my job, Minister."*

Minister: *"Could we switch places for a while?"*

Slave: *"You mean, I move to the prime table and you stay with Valeria?"*

Minister: *"Exactly."*

Slave: *"Okay, but I cannot promise that I can make them dance when you play the piano."*

Just a few weeks later, the minister was appointed to become a boss within a big international organization. His head of office called to ask me whether I would like to apply for a job on his team. I accepted and we stayed together for almost ten years.

I never dared to ask him whether he really liked all these important jobs he had – and he never asked me again to trade places.

The Flying Ambassador

It is still an open question whether mental toughness is primarily a developed characteristic or has a genetic basis. Anyway, an important number of scientists believe that extensive sport experience supports the development of skills that are considered to be essential for professional success. In this view there is no better way than sports to learn realistic optimism, confidence, perseverance, handling pressure and resilience.

The case of Erik Vander Castle was special. Sure, he was something like a sports madman but most of all he seemed to be addicted to sports that moved him up in the air. He placed a huge trampoline in his garden and of course he loved parachuting as much as kite-surfing. In terms of the mental-toughness theory however, the most valuable experiences undoubtedly stemmed from paragliding. In Austria he hung more than three hours on the top of a tree somewhere in the woods before the fire brigade had finally found him to cut him off - a unique opportunity for Erik to develop his resilience and will to survive. At another occasion in Africa, Erik was arrested by an armed anti-espionage patrol right after landing. The rest of the day he spent in a windowless interrogation room with two anti-espionage officers and developed the skill to remain optimistic and friendly, even under adverse conditions (the unfriendly guys repeatedly showed him their guns and did not want to buy his story that he was just flying around).

The development of skills was, however, only half of the story. The other half was whether they were relevant. Erik worked with a big international organization and the big international organization was at least as special as Erik, although in a different way. The most required skill was to remain optimistic and friendly even under adverse conditions (superiors in the big international organization do not tend to show their guns, but a good number of them could be equally unfriendly, unpredictable and suspicious). Erik sometimes felt that keeping control was even more difficult than in the interrogation room, but finally he succeeded. After a number of quite fussy internal jobs he was tasked to open the liaison office of the big international organization in La Habana.

His boss pushed him through against 27 other candidates. In the selection board he had praised Erik's diplomatic skills in iridescent colors and underscored how important they would be for the job. The boss was a very busy man with no time to chat with his staff about their hobbies or passions and he was also unaware of the recent academic research dealing with the transfer of skills from sports to work. It was therefore not surprising that he had no imagination of the necessities required to keep Erik's skills alive.

We listen in to a telephone conversation between Lieutenant Alberto Ramirez and Colonel Joaquin Sanchez. Alberto was married to a language teacher who had emigrated some time ago from former East Germany. Lieutenant Ramirez was therefore perfectly able to understand German and English and once the particulars were known, Colonel Sanchez arranged also an intensive course in Dutch for him. Some weeks later, Erik Vander Castle hired Alberto as a concierge for his private residence in La Habana.

It was a nice sunny day in September. When they began to talk about Erik Vander Castle Alberto used the code name "Emilio" for him.

Saturday: 9:00 a.m.

Alberto (in Spanish): *"How are you this morning, Colonel Sanchez?"*

Colonel Sanchez: *"I just woke up. I think I need a coffee. And you?"*

Alberto: *"Busy. Emilio went jogging at 6 o'clock with the dog. As always."*

Colonel Sanchez: *"And? Did he get in touch with somebody?"*

Alberto: *"No he didn't, Colonel. As long as he is taking that dog along a normal person would not dare to get near him. Emilio calls him Lion and in fact Lion is almost as big as a real lion. It looks very much like he would not even mind fighting with one, you know."*

Alberto hated the job. Emilio was running like hell and Alberto was not really a morning person. Alberto's first idea had been to hire one or two people from the athletics team to take over Emilio's running tour, but Colonel Sanchez needed them to observe other members of the athletics team. The dog was Lieutenant Alberto Ramirez' last chance to get back his good night's rest. If Alberto could make Sanchez believe that the dog was much more effective in cushioning Emilio from objectionable contacts than any observer he would have a fair chance.

Colonel Sanchez: *"It is a Rhodesian Ridgeback, Ramirez. In former times Ridgebacks were indeed used to hunt lions. Male species do measure up to 69.5 cm. The average lifespan is 10.25 years."*

Lieutenant Alberto Ramirez wondered how many more people might have the pleasure of daily conversations with Colonel Sanchez. Estimated against his knowledge on details, the number was certainly at least in the double digits. Alberto started to worry that these lion dogs might only appear a little bit too big and were only nasty to lions. Other sources could inform Colonel Sanchez that they could be extremely nice to little children, elderly people and dissidents. Instantly, Alberto decided to extend the phasing-in period of his new plan. He needed at least one or two more trial runs. His first spontaneous idea was to deliberately leave out the word "dog" when he was talking about the lion dog.

Alberto: *"At the moment the lion is kept within the boundary fence of the tennis court. Emilio has another smaller dog which is actually on heat. Of course the lion got wind of it. If you ask me, he could go mad at any time. Nobody in the whole world could stop that animal when it gets out of there."*

Colonel Sanchez: *"The other dog is a cross-breed between a cross-breed mother and a Pinscher. Obviously, Rhodesian Ridgebacks are much less picky than their owners. But why is this relevant, Ramirez?"*

Alberto: *"Emilio has invited the President of the Association for a tennis match. The match is supposed to take place at 4:00 p.m. It will be interesting to see how he will set the preferences."*

Colonel Sanchez: *"Indeed. Keep me posted!"*

Saturday: 1:15 p.m.

Alberto: *"How is the day, Colonel Sanchez?"*

Colonel Sanchez: *"Not too bad. We are actually in the garden having lunch. But how is yours?"*

Alberto: *"Busy. I had to take off the rope above the trampoline."*

Colonel Sanchez: *"Brand name Tarzan. 4.75 external diameters. Made in Switzerland."*

Alberto (wondering): *"It may be that one, indeed. Anyway, Emilio asked me to remove it. But I am quite sure that I have to put it up again very soon."*

Colonel Sanchez: *"What makes you believe that?"*

Alberto: *"Emilio might not want to give the impression to the President of the Association that he is a bit special in terms of sports."*

Colonel Sanchez: *"Maybe he is just tired."*

Alberto: *"Emilio and tired? With all the respect I owe you, Colonel Sanchez, this guy is never tired."*

Colonel Sanchez (frowning): *"So he will continue to jump from the trampoline up to the rope, grab it and swing on it?"*

Alberto: *"Upside down, Colonel. And sometimes he layaways between the trees."*

Colonel Sanchez: *"Exactly 4 meters and 27 cm above the ground."*

Alberto: *"By the way, Colonel Sanchez. The two trees in the garden to fix the rope are quite high. 4 meters something might not be the end of the story and I have no head for heights. If Emilio continues to receive important visitors at his residence I should at least have a ladder."*

Saturday: 4:55 p.m.

Alberto: *"I hope I did not wake you up, Colonel Sanchez."*

Colonel Sanchez: *"No problem. I have set the clock for 5 anyway. How are you Ramirez?"*

Alberto: *"Busy. The tennis match developed quite dramatically."*

Colonel Sanchez: *"That is surprising. Emilio was runner up at the tennis championship of Southern Limburg in 1987. On the other hand, the President of the Association had never appeared at official tournaments. He had only played at an invitation tournament at the Club Med of Agadir where he had been eliminated already in the second round. "*

Alberto: *"Emilio was clearly the better player and won the first set by 6:1. But that was not the point. You remem-*

ber the lion, Colonel Sanchez? Emilio tried to lock him in the house. But it did not work that well. The animal was so nervous because of the cross-breed-Pinscher. After some first collateral damage, Emilio had to drag him back to the tennis court and tied him to the fence behind the baseline."

Colonel Sanchez: "You are making me curious."

Alberto: "At the outset everything went well. Of course the lion would have liked to snap the ball, but Emilio played well in front of the baseline and returned all the balls before the lion could come into play."

Colonel Sanchez: "And how did the President do?"

Alberto: "I wonder whether he is not even more ambitious than Emilio. He blamed the court for the loss of the first set. He complained that there were many more holes at his side and that was why many balls have bounced badly. He insisted on changing sides."

Colonel Sanchez: "You mean he chose to play in front of the lion, just because…? Now you are making me really curious, Lieutenant Ramirez."

Alberto: "The President of the Association was quite focused on the ball, I must say. Unfortunately Emilio had lobbed him after an attack to the net and he ran backwards to retrieve it. Unfortunately, the lion was also equally focused on the ball."

Colonel Sanchez: *"And who got it first?"*

Alberto: *"I do not know where the President has seen this. He thought the best choice was to return the ball between his legs."*

Colonel Sanchez: *"Very demanding strike. The first player who did that was Yannick Noah against Mats Wilander in 1983."*

Alberto: *"The lion arrived just when the ball was just 20 cm in front of the Presidents balls, Colonel Sanchez. And he arrived with a lot of speed…."*

Colonel Sanchez did not want to listen to the end of the story. He wished Alberto a good evening and hung up. He had to get ready for his afternoon drink at his favorite Salsa bar. It was only 150 meters away but of course he would use the car.

Sports and the ultimate consequences were for guys like Lieutenant Ramirez. He was the boss.

Helping Hayek

Why can't even the most sophisticated football experts predict the result of a match? Why can't even the best investment bankers and market analysts properly gauge the prospects for the future value of a company? It looks very much as though we neither have a guarantee that stocks could not halve in value within months, nor that the underdog would never win against the champion. If we go a step further we may conclude that the existence of stock exchange markets (where market participants trade on the basis of different expectations) may serve as a proof that we do not know much about the future of markets. It sounds strange, but parts of economic science seem to conclude that market prices are somewhat an exception. This caused a Nobel Prize winner to stand up, Friedrich Hayek. He held the knowledge that would be necessary to prove that predicting prices cannot be captured by a single scientist. As relevant information is spread among millions of market participants, predicting future prices was just a mere presumption of knowledge.

Hayek died in 1992 but he had left a number of supporters. One of these supporters was me. At one point in time, a number of very bright people came to the conclusion that it would be a good idea to use price theory in the application of antitrust law and merger control. At the same time I held a job in the economic department of a big international organization.

The envisaged policy change towards more economics in antitrust law raised strong expectations from economists of a substantial increase of well paid expertise to be provided by economists to cartel offices and courts. It goes without saying that in this particular business environment, Hayek's skepticism of the "presumption" of knowledge was not very popular and neither was I, Hayek's loyal supporter. During a presentation a very excited post-modern economist snarled at me about how an economist could ever put so much energy in warning against an application of economics. I hesitated for a moment. But then I told the audience the true story of "Helping Hayek".

In the 1960s Friedrich Hayek was a professor in Freiburg, a middle sized German town at the edge of the Black Forest. The University was very proud to host such a famous scientist and so was the city of Freiburg. After his retirement Professor Hayek accepted the offer to stay in town. He lived in a beautiful house in the Urachstrasse and was allowed to keep his office at the university. Fifteen years later I became the assistant to the successor of Professor Hayek who had received the honor to take over Hayek's institute in 1967.

Professor Hayek was already in his eighties but from time to time he showed up at the university, mainly to deal with the many invitations he received from all over the world. On one occasion he had accepted an invitation from Milan. The secretary asked me whether I would be happy to pick him up from the Urachstrasse and help him to the station. As elderly people are sometimes afraid that they might miss their train, I took the pleasure to spend an hour and a half with the Nobel prize winner in the dingy "Bahnhofswirtschaft" of Freiburg. I asked him a couple of things related to his academic work. Actually, I do not remember anymore which question it was. He looked at me and said in his lovely Austrian accent:

"Hob i des wiakli g'schriebn?" (Did I really write that?)

Within a second my confidence broke down into pieces. I thought that I have misread or at least completely misunderstood the master and I did not dare to raise any further professional questions. The remaining time we talked about some details and I felt relieved when the train had left the station. You may imagine that I was very surprised when one week later I found a card from Professor Hayek in my letter box. He had invited me to a personal reception at tea time in the Urachstrasse. I am not sure whether I was much more entertaining during our tea conversation than in the Bahnhofswirtschaft. But I still remember that he showed me around in his huge library and invited me to select one of his books. There were so many of them but as for me it was not very difficult: I chose the original edition of "The Road to Serfdom", the legendary masterpiece of 1944. Hayek seemed to be satisfied. He smiled, took the book from my hands and signed it with the words:

"Thanks for your help. F.A. von Hayek "

After I ended my story I waited a couple of seconds before I turned to the excited economist and said: *"You see, Professor Hayek thanked me for helping him with "The Road to Serfdom" even though it was published before my birth. You may now understand why I am happy to defend his views after his death."*

The Philosophy of the Organigram

"Life is unfair – but not always to your disadvantage." Lezney sat in his big office chair, recalling the famous quote from J.F. Kennedy. Actually, he felt that he could not agree more.

The government had appointed the Big Boss for another five years to represent the country in the big international organization. All parties of the coalition had been keen to fill the post with a member from their own party, so the re-appointment of the Big Boss was received as a big surprise. At the time of the decision the former head of cabinet had already prepared a parachute to land safely at the top level of the administration. The even bigger surprise was however that the Big Boss asked Joe to take over. Instead of returning to a back seat at the national ministry from where he was detached for the period of the first mandate, he moved to the huge office next to the Big Boss. He did not believe it before he read it black on white on the big name tag in front of the door: Joe Lezney, Head of Cabinet.

Joe Lezney was neither a passionate networker nor one of the guys who never seem to get tired of trying to be in the spotlight of superiors at any possible occasion. Joe was a rather calm fellow. The Big Boss had a preference for people he already knew and he liked Joe for his objectivity and un-agitated working style. A number of people had been keen to get the job. Joe was aware that Gaylord Scrub was deeply disappointed. Due to new rules to foster gender balance he was not even considered as deputy (the job had to be filled by a female candidate). Scrub was extremely ambitious but unlike some similar species he could not hide it. He was not very popular and the people who worked with him said that Scrub was so keen that he would even consider sex change surgery to get the job.

On top of that the prime minister had insisted on nominating an official from his own private office for a job in the cabinet. Lezney could imagine how fiercely these two fellows would fight to get at least the unofficial number three position. That this simply did not matter in any formal sense was irrelevant. Joe would soon have to send out an organigram and one of the two would read his name below the other. And most probably start a big fight which could impede the working climate for months or even longer.

Joe dialed the number of Alison, his deputy. She had worked with several cabinets before and gained some experience with sensitive personnel issues.

Joe: *"Alison, when do we have to send out our organigram to the President?"*

Alison: *"By the end of this week. But we are almost there. Apart from some details, the dossiers are allocated to the team members."*

Joe: *"Very good. But I will still have to write the names in order. Do you have a suggestion?"*

Alison: *"I have not thought about it. The normal procedure is to rank the members according to their grade. That would be perfectly objective."*

Joe: *"I am afraid that this might not work. Think of the new guy the government sent us."*

Alison: *"Oh my dear! He is quite young. The administration attributed a very low grade to him."*

Joe: *"If we put him on the bottom of the list, he'll call the prime minister. And the prime minister will call the Big Boss and ask him whether we have lost our minds to put his man in fourth."*

Alison: *"You are right. We are in politics. So we have to act like politicians."*

Joe: *"So what are we going to do about this, Alison?"*

Alison: *"We can rank Prime Minister's darling number three and Gaylord Scrub number four. I think Scrub is in the office now. I will try to convince him that such a piece of paper is not the end of the world."*

Joe: *"Don't be too optimistic, Alison. It might very well be the end of the world. Good luck."*

Joe Lezney hung up and took a look at the office's meeting table. The outgoing head of cabinet used to chair the daily meetings sitting at the front end near his desk. Gaylord Scrub was always the first who appeared and saved himself the seat next to the deputy who sat to the right of the boss. If the deputy was absent Scrub immediately grabbed his chair. Joe had watched this spectacle over the years and concluded that Scrub must be close to a maniac. When Joe was appointed as the new Head he deliberately chose the place at the opposite end of the table to chair the meetings. He was not surprised that it took no longer than two days before Scrub started to move in his direction.

At this very moment Alison came rushing into the office. Joe noticed that she looked a bit desperate.

Joe: *"That was a short meeting, Alison."*

Alison: *"Mister Scrub simply took the view that the young baby boy will never be above him on the list and that there would be nothing to discuss."*

Joe: *"And what did he say to the 'not-the-end-of-the-world-philosophy'?"*

Alison: *"We did not really get to philosophy. He started to yell at me and shouted that he will raise the issue with the Big Boss."*

Joe: *"Not a good start for us, Alison."*

Alison: *"Indeed. But even the best philosophy does not help against the power of genes. According to some people moral philosophy only exists because the human genes are generally immoral."*

Joe: *"In that case I will have to talk to the Big Boss, before our friend Gaylord does. When will the Big Boss return from his conference?"*

Alison: *"Tomorrow around noon."*

Joe: *"Wonderful. I have a visitor around that time. Would you please take that over for me and ask Scrub to go with you to that meeting?"*

Alison (smiling): *"I am sure he will like that. But what will you say to the Big Boss?"*

Joe: *"I don't know yet. But I may consider deepening your philosophical approach."*

Joe Lezney handed the draft organigram to the Big Boss. It looked different from all versions in the cabinet's history and also different from anything the big international organization had ever seen before. Instead of ranking the members below each other, Joe had put them in groups of two. Below him and Alison, Scrub and Baby Boy shared the second line shoulder to shoulder. In this vein the organigram looked like a square but, despite some last minute efforts by Alison with the layout, unfortunately a bit stocky.

The Big Boss was a literate man and interested in all kinds of things. Joe was sure that the explanations he had prepared for this unique organigram innovation would impress him.

Big Boss (he had not yet looked at the list): *"Are all members happy with the attribution of tasks?"*

Joe: *"In general, yes. We will, however, encounter a review after some time."*

Big Boss (looking at the paper) *"But what is this?!"*

Joe: *"The draft organigram for your cabinet. We have incorporated some knowledge on the philosophy of shapes."*

Big Boss (frowning): *"Interesting."*

Joe: *"Shapes can be open or closed, angular or round, big or small. Shapes can be organic or inorganic. Each shape can communicate its own meaning and message."*

Big Boss: *"I see. This is what you meant by philosophy."*

Joe: *"Circles for example have no beginning or end. They represent the eternal whole. Circles protect, they endure and they restrict. They confine what's within. And what is without."*

Big Boss (pointing to the paper): *"But this looks rather like a square."*

Joe: *"Indeed. Squares are stable. They suggest honesty. They have right angles and represent order, security, equality and peacefulness."*

Big Boss: *"Quite innovative shape, indeed. It has, however, the disadvantage that you can barely read the relevant responsibilities without using a magnifying glass. There seems not to be enough space for two honest and peaceful cabinet members in just one line of a normal piece of paper."*

Joe: *"We are still working on the layout."*

Big Boss: *"May I be honest with you, Joe?"*

Joe: *"Of course."*

Big Boss: *"I have seen quite a number of psychological dra-*

mas. And this looks like one. But you can't solve the problem like this. The next fight will be about whom of the two will have his name standing on the left side of the page. We read from left to right. And as you are the Head of Cabinet the list starts logically with you on the left side. Do you get me?"

Joe: *"I got you."*

Big Boss (laughing): *"I like the organigram, Joe. Keep it as it is. In politics we have to square the circle almost every day. Our organigram shows that we already have a philosophy."*

Joe: *"And where do I put Scrub? Left or right?"*

Big Boss: *"You put him at the bottom, what else? Once he has seen his name there, he will protest and you can move him up to the right of our new young man. You will see, he will be extremely happy."*

Joe (smiling): *"You mean, it is possible to square the circle, but it needs two rounds?"*

Big Boss: *"Indeed. But don't tell anyone."*

Mauro's Migraine

Niccolo was in a bad mood. It was one of his assets that he managed to smile when he was angry. But the trick only worked when he was with his superiors. When he was talking to other people, one of his favorite words was "idiot". This time he had kept control. When Marion told him the news, he had not yelled that Mauro was an idiot. But he had been very close to it.

Actually, Niccolo was just about to reduce the number of superiors, which was his foremost professional objective. He was determined and strategic. Just as a good chess player never thinks only of a single move but rather of two or three ahead, he needed to clear the territory before he could be appointed to the next hierarchy level. His strategy had been to build up strong loyalties with some of the members of the team. It was essential to have a sufficient number of allies who would tell him proactively what was going on after he had moved up. If he was successful he would be able to act against any attempt by his successor to side-line him.

From this inner circle he had expected slavish obedience. On the other hand he was prepared to help them and discriminate against the few others who occasionally dared to challenge his views. His favourite functional currency had been the dossiers that involved international meetings, the visibility he was willing to grant towards the top management and, of course, the amount of information he was passing on to individual team members. In the past months Niccolo had made considerable progress. His deputy Marion Etten was following him blindly and he was able to bring his two closest allies into the key positions. Furthermore, two out of the three team members he had on his personal blacklist had already left the unit.

The event of their departure had, however, been a bit delicate since the two delinquents had left under rather dramatic circumstances. While the first one was so upset that he left without saying a word or an invite to the usual goodbye drink, number two suffered from depression and was not expected to return to work for at least a few months. He hoped that the HR department bought his story that these events had nothing to do with his management style but it couldn't be overlooked that the reputation of the social climate in his team was doubtful and he had failed over a long time to recruit a new secretary. HR people were the pain in his neck. Most recently they had persuaded the Director General to issue a note in which he publicly stated that management skills would be predominant selection criteria for management jobs. Niccolo wondered why this had to be stated but he sensed that he had to be careful. He knew that the issue with Mauro was somewhat a consequence of his own dirty strategy. Marion Etten also knew it. But as usual she would not say anything.

The unit was located on one of the top floors of the building. However, there was also a small office far away from the others just above the huge main street where all the traffic from the highway rolled on six lanes into downtown. From the small window to the street level the linear distance was no more than five meters. For people who wanted to open a window for fresh air or were sensitive to noise and air pollution the office was the ultimate nightmare. But Niccolo would not be Niccolo if he had not deliberately used the first occasion to allocate the office to one of his blacklist candidates. When the angry fellow finally left, Niccolo happily recruited Mauro who was from the outset a strong candidate for his inner circle. But the only office space that was available was just the one that the delinquent had recently left in anger.

When Mauro saw his new office he became furious. Niccolo asked him to be patient until his own promotion was through and promised that his alliance and loyalty would finally pay off. But Mauro did not want to listen. Marion Etten had just informed Niccolo that Mauro had appeared in her office and had insisted on instantly getting out of "the cell".

Niccolo (loudly): *"What an…!"* (Niccolo did not finish the sentence. This was the moment reported earlier in which he had controlled himself).

Mrs. Etten: *"Mauro said that he gets a migraine in his office. He also said that he will not be able to come to work anymore until we have found a better place for him."*

Niccolo: *"My new post is already published and the procedure will not take any longer than two or three months. The first thing I will do is to get him out of there. Why can't he just wait until my promotion is through?"*

Mrs. Etten: *"A migraine is maybe just a migraine, Niccolo."*

Niccolo: *"Bullshit. He can keep the window closed and turn off the ventilation so that the smog can't get in. He knows that it would be only for a short period of time – he can endure it. My office also looks out to the main street and I have also survived."*

Mrs. Etten: *"This is exactly what I told him. But he replied that your office is six or seven times bigger than his, so there is more air to breathe. Most of all, he stated that your office is some levels higher from the street. He strongly believes that this would make some difference."*

Niccolo looked at the photomontage which had been a Christmas present from his wife. The picture was showing the most famous emperors of Rome sitting together at a table. He had placed it on the wall just behind his desk. From the meeting table he could see his empty chair just in front of these important men. Occasionally he liked to take a look, most of all when the situation required taking hard decisions. It felt good when he remembered that guys like Augustus or Caesar did not rule half of the world just because they were particularly fair or emphatic: these heroes of history were determined to increase their power and ready to eliminate anybody who could be in the way.

Niccolo: *"How about an exchange with Maverick?"*

Marion Etten was afraid that Niccolo would come up with Steven Maverick. She would not publicly admit but she felt a lot of respect for him. Maverick did not bow at all to Niccolo or to anyone else. He tried to build upon his independent technical judgment. But most of all he was a friendly man who had seen a lot of things and had still kept his sense of humor. Unfortunately he had always been the number one candidate on Niccolo's blacklist. Now that the other two had left, Marion Etten had seen it coming.

Niccolo: *"Could we find a rule that the natural choice would be Steven Maverick?"*

Mrs. Etten: *"That is not so easy from the outset. He is closer to 60 than Mauro is to 40. He is therefore also in a much higher grade. And as you know it is normally the other way around: once somebody gets to a qualifying grade he instantly needs a bigger office with more windows. So it would look a bit strange if we would reverse the rule."*

Niccolo: *"We have to build on the migraine, not on age or grade. This case is a medical urgency."*

Mrs. Etten: *"But that does not yet answer the question why Maverick in particular should give up his office to move to the ce… I mean to the office on level 2."*

Niccolo: *"But it reduces the number of candidates. Do you remember the last occasion I moved Maverick to the suburbs?"*

Mrs. Etten: *"I do. He was very unhappy that he was separated from his favorite colleagues."*

Niccolo: *"But it was a courtyard office, Marion! A courtyard office! Don't you understand? The treatment of Mauro's migraine does not only require that he gets away from the street, he needs a courtyard office! That's it! It reduces the number to … (he looked at the plan) … exactly six candidates."*

Marion could not believe her ears. There were lots of offices which did not look out to the noisy main street and all of them were on the upper floor. Furthermore, Mauro had occupied one of these offices in his former job and never complained. Niccolo's fantasy obviously had no limits.

She was keen to hear what he would suggest to choose Maverick from the remaining six.

Mrs. Etten: *"But how do you want to reduce the choice from six to one? Still he is by far the most senior and the oldest."*

Niccolo: *"Exactly."*

Mrs. Etten: *"I am not sure that I understand."*

Niccolo: *"You see, from a man at his age and experience we may expect that he would not take such a move so much to heart. He should go ahead and set an example for the younger colleagues. You will find the right words, I am sure."*

Mrs. Etten (surprised): *"I beg your pardon? Did you say me?"*

Niccolo: *"You are my deputy and in charge of the personnel, aren't you?"*

Mrs. Etten: *"I think it may be better if you ask your assistant. She could stay a bit vague in the messages as to why he was chosen and if he happens to embark on a defense campaign you can still say that she had got it a little bit wrong and the conversation was just meant to be the start of a wider consultation process involving a number of other colleagues."*

Marion Etten was not particularly proud of herself. As it seemed, working with Niccolo rubbed off on her. But she had no reason to dirty her hands and, like the boss, she found a way to pass it on.

Niccolo (with a smile): *"Okay, Marion. Instruct her. But she has to wait until next Monday."*

Mrs. Etten: *"But this is the carnival week and we are both on vacation."*

Niccolo: *"Bingo. But how could we otherwise explain that the assistant has to bring over the message?"*

Mrs. Etten (slightly shaking her head): *"Indeed."*

Niccolo: *"By the way, I am not going on vacation. I have cancelled in order to visit a training course on personnel management. The HR people are very keen to see the attendance certificate before someone is applying for the top jobs. You should do that as well."*

Mrs. Etten: *"I will, Niccolo. I will."*

Hank and the Promotion Game

Hank van Broudworst and Mike Miller crossed the court-yard to enter the cafeteria. Hank had always looked a bit lost in the past and as an alleged underperformer people were used to look down on him. But surprisingly enough Hank's mood had recently improved. Two colleagues of his unit had started to look after him. They arranged fresh flowers in his office, they bought his favorite newspapers and, which was the most visible, invited him regularly to the cafeteria. Hank ordered at least two pieces of cake at the sales counter and Miller paid them without objection. After Hank had finished the first portion Miller discretely pulled out his handset and sent a secret message. One minute later Bodo Ludens appeared to take over. In this vein, Hank spent half of the mornings in friendly company, something which he had not experienced before. Of course, everybody was wondering why Hank was suddenly so much "en vogue". On the other hand, it was widely known that Miller was very ambitious and many people who saw them together could not avoid the feeling that there must be an agenda.

Indeed, the big international organization had just introduced a new regime for the promotion of its officials. Mike Miller held a masters degree in economics and was the first who understood all implications. He found out that the new promotion system was operating on the basis of a zero-sum game. A zero–sum game is a mathematical representation of a situation in which a participant's gain (or loss) is exactly balanced by the losses (or gains) of the other participant(s). If the total gains of the participants are added up and the total losses are subtracted, they will sum to zero. Miller concluded that nothing would be more important for his future than having the unhappy Hank van Broudworst on his side.

Miller also understood that zero-sum games are qualified as "strictly competitive". And if the new promotion game was strictly competitive, successful players had to be, too. Miller was determined to fight by all means. The game was, however, rather complex and Miller was not sure whether his mathematical skills would be sufficient to identify the dominant strategy. While for example in a zero-sum card game like the German "Skat" the number of players is limited to three, the promotion game involved more than 20.000 players. Furthermore, the successful candidate had to accumulate his promotion points on a year to year basis until finally he would reach a promotion threshold. The problem was however, that the threshold was a moving target – nobody could tell whether the number of accumulated points which were sufficient to promote a player in year one would be sufficient for another player in year two.

Mike Miller accepted that he would have to considerably reduce the complexity of the game. He made substantial progress when a friend who worked in the administration told him that the internal guidelines called managers to respect the rules of the zero-sum game in every division and every unit of the organization. Miller concluded that his individual score would not so much depend on his performance but rather on who else was with him in the same game: in a unit with ten Einsteins no single Einstein would be in the position to get much more than average points while any one-eyed could achieve a wonderful score if only he was lucky enough to work with a bunch of the blind. Actually, this was Miller's most important finding and, at the same time, the reason why Hank van Broudworst's life had so suddenly changed.

While others still kept on complaining about the new regime, Miller started to implement his policy. He knew that Hank felt desperate because he had been treated like a useless twerp for quite a while. Miller's first priority was to keep Hank amused so that he would abstain from looking for a new job. Together with Bodo Ludens who was equally ambitious and immediately co-operated with Miller, he launched a secret fund which was due to finance the van Broudworst activities. They did however not only sponsor flowers, newspapers and Hank's daily ramble at the cake buffet – Miller and Ludens also kept an eye on other colleagues, rumor had, were underperforming. Miller kept a list in the top drawer of his desk, ready to recommend quite a number of candidates if the manager would ask for proposals to fill up a new vacancy.

The only thing left to do was to explain to the manager how he could exploit the opportunities of the new gamble. Since nobody could imagine that Hank van Broudworst would ever be promoted, there was no particular reason to have mercy on him. Instead of accumulating the points needed to ensure a zero sum by scoring all other members slightly below the average (which would be received as an unfriendly act and perish motivation), the dominant strategy was to identify a sacrificial lamb. Fortunately such a lamb was already there. Miller was very positive that he could convince the boss that only a shattering point-hammering for Hank would pave the way for rapid promotions.

Miller had proven that he could identify a "win-win" situation even under complex conditions. Hank might perhaps recently have gained some weight but without any doubt he visibly felt much better now. Since the administration had announced that there will be new opportunities for early retirement, Hank actually pro-actively made up his mind, an asset which had never mentioned in one of his appraisal reports. Nevertheless, he had not yet developed a particular plan how to get a series of devastating scores he would need to become eligible for the program. The manager of the unit was not known as an ultimate risk taker and would certainly shy away from any action which could turn in something like trouble or a court case.

As he sat down with Miller, Hank felt very much like talking about his plan and that he would need at least two or three consecutive knock down reports. But he did not dare. His new friends were so nice to him and in the last months something like a long lasting friendship might have started. If he would tell about his plan, Miller and Ludens might blame him that he was prepared to leave them alone in the frosty coldness of the big international organization. As long as the early retirement plan was not successful he would have to carry on working here. In the worst case Miller and Ludens would immediately turn away from him and his openness could take bitter revenge.

Van Broudworst looked warmly at Miller who just had pulled out his mobile to send out an SMS message. At this very moment, he felt that he would never manage to tell Miller the truth about his intentions. He decided that he had to develop his own game plan to achieve the scores he needed.

Tennis with the Boss

Team building activities are part of modern personnel management. There are a number of good reasons to foster team building and nowadays, hundreds of commercial providers offer specialized programs. Among the activities offered in such events playing "games" ranks high. The optimists (who are normally located in the HR unit) usually hope that selfish guys with big egos will no longer be selfish after a new experience of happiness in a co-operative group game and turn into effective team players. The incorrigible pessimists, however, suppose that just a little day of playing "pass the clap" or "whose shoes" will never be enough to wipe out certain testosterone levels. These pessimists would bet that the half-life of any of these supposed effects were no longer than 10 minutes.

At the time, the Big Boss decided to host his own private tennis tournament, the art of teambuilding was in its early stages. The Big Boss was very enthusiastic about sports and happy to organize the finals in the park near his house. It was most probably a rather unintended side effect, but, narrated retrospectively, the Big Boss became a front runner of modern personnel management (tennis tournaments are still indispensable to foster team spirit in some parts of the big international organization). Without any doubt, his tournament offered an interesting sample of test people. Almost all invitees had accepted and as only cabinet members and some big shots from the head office were invited, a layer of testosterone hovered above the courts.

Tennis is a very selective, competitive game. Gentlemen like Mr. McEnroe and Mr. Connors occasionally over-stated the importance of the umpire, but generally it is fair to say that in 99% of all cases the better player wins. There is nobody else to blame for a devastating whitewash and even the most obsessive overachievers have to con-cede that mere ambition is not sufficient to compensate for a lousy talent. Future generations of tennis tournaments organized by the big international organization corrected the selective nature of the game by building teams to play against each other, thereby putting the outstanding players deliberately in a team with the hopeless bush leaguers so that they had no chance to win.

However, the tennis tournament of the Big Boss was a "sin-gles men" competition and based on the blunt knock out system. David Egg was in charge of the draw. He had not been keen on taking over the job and cursed his stupidity that he had told the others about his participation in the internal tournament of his tennis club. In Egg's analysis, organizing the tournament offered no opportunities to achieve additional merit points for his career. On the other hand, he saw the red light - a wrong draw could cost him all chances. If he were to be unlucky enough to set up a match that would eliminate the Big Boss at the early stage of the tournament, he would be done for.

David Egg felt very serious about it and worked hard to get it right. He retrieved basic information from all available sources and ranked the participants alongside estimated performance levels. His second move was to do his best to manipulate the course of the competition to the advantage of the Big Boss. While normally the best player is seeded number one and the second best is placed at the opposite end of the draw (to avoid that they have to play against each other before the final), Egg seeded all players he considered to be competitive in the upper half of the draw and placed the presumably hopeless rest with the Big Boss in the other. Egg hoped that in this way he had eliminated all serious competitors for the Big Boss to reach the final.

David Egg was completely overwhelmed when he learnt that the new speech writer of the Big Boss had a history of rather successful tennis tournaments. At first he thought that it was just a bad joke invented by his colleagues to tease him. Egg was nevertheless alarmed. He knew that the first match he had set up for the Big Boss was unfortunately against just this new colleague and his nightmare could become reality. Egg discussed several crisis management plans with his closest allies. The view of the majority was that David should discuss the issue with the new speech writer – in fact he was in the same boat as David and would probably co-operate.

David had invited Franz Fechner for lunch in a restaurant somewhat away from the offices. After the soup he came to the point.

David: *"Is it really true that you are an excellent tennis player?"*

Franz: *"I don't know. Everything is relative in this sport. And*

*it has been some time now. My new sport is speech writing –
at the moment around three or four per week."*

David: *"But you are still playing at a decent level, aren't
you?"*

Franz: *"As I told you – everything is relative."*

David: *"Did you see the draw for our tournament?"*

Franz: *"I think that I have all the luck."*

David suddenly realized the weakness of his strategy.
Franz was still a sportsman and had only recently joined
the big international organization. He could not yet imagine that someone would manipulate competitions. David
gave up and they turned away from the topic of the tennis
tournament. His last hope was that Franz would realize
the severity of his situation and draw the right conclusion himself. If he were in Franz's shoes, Egg would have
simulated an injury or even invented the cause of death of
his grandmother but he would certainly never appear on
the tennis court to eliminate his boss in round one of his
tennis tournament.

The match took place at the premises of the big international organization (the courts in the park were reserved
for the finals). David, who had initially planned to watch
all matches of the Big Boss, decided to stay in his office -
but had placed a secret spy to inform him on the standings.
The Big Boss himself was a bit confused when his speech

writer appeared with one of these big bags the tennis pros normally use to carry the dozens of rackets they need for a big tournament. The surprise was complete when Franz selected among a number of obviously equal looking rackets by testing the tension of the strings.

The match itself was rather short. David's spy later reported that it did not make sense to hustle to the club house in order to call him as agreed after the first set because the match might have been over before he could return (mobile phones were not yet on the market). Franz was not nasty at all, he played his balls nicely more or less in the middle of the court and at much less than his maximum speed and spin. He was just far too good for a normal amateur player, and so he was, of course, too good for the Big Boss. When they changed sides for the last time, Franz explained that he had played some international tournaments and that he had even played a match against the German tennis legend Boris Becker.

The following morning, the Big Boss received a visitor. David and Franz were asked to attend. As they waited outside, David barely spoke a word. He did not feel very enthusiastic about meeting the Big Boss in the aftermath of his defeat during round 1 of his own tennis tournament. When they were called in, he tried to hide a bit behind Franz who was quite a tall fellow. To David's huge surprise the Big Boss was in a very good mood and introduced his team members. Speech writers are normally invisible people, but he seemed to be particularly proud of Franz.

"This is Franz Fechner. Yesterday, I convinced myself that he is an excellent tennis player."

The visitor stared at the Big Boss and at Franz and did not understand why this was relevant. *"He once played against Boris Becker."*

David saw how the visitor started to really wonder.

"Franz lost in three sets. Imagine if he had won – then Boris Becker would be in my cabinet."